Spoinkers Christmas Wish

Cheri Seward

ISBN: 978-0-9994535-0-6

Spoinkers Christmas Wish

For my three children, you are always my inspiration.
Thank you to all who supported my dream!

It was an ordinary October day, well, ordinary for the North Pole.

Santa's reindeer were getting ready for winter and needed plenty of exercise. After Christmas, the reindeer take a break. As you can see, they have added on a few pounds. You can't eat oats with sprinkles every day.

Reindeer training is next to an open pen that's home to Santa's pigs. Santa is fond of his pigs and enjoys chatting with them on his morning walks with Mrs. Claus.

There is one particular pig named Spoinkers, who always gives the same morning greeting.

"Good morning, Santa and Mrs. Claus! It's a beautiful day today. Not a cloud in the sky and a perfect day for a pig to learn how to fly." Spoinker's greeting made Santa and Mrs. Claus giggle every time.

Spoinkers has many friends, and eats oats with sprinkles every day, just like the reindeer.

Santa would say, "Keep eating your sprinkles, Spoinkers, and some day you may fly." The reindeer would say "pigs don't fly."

Not only did Spoinkers want to fly, he dreamed of pulling Santa's sleigh. Every day he would ask, with hopes that one day Santa would say yes.

Well, that "one day" came last October.

Santa was in a jolly good mood while walking with Mrs. Claus. Spoinkers offered his usual, "It's a beautiful day today. Not a cloud in the sky and a perfect day for a pig to learn how to fly".

Only this time, Santa laid a finger aside his nose and said, "It is a perfect day for a pig to learn how to fly."

Spoinkers was confused when Santa didn't giggle and was surprised when his feet started to feel funny and tingle.

Spoinkers yelled, "Santa, is today the day?" Santa smiled as Spoinker's tail started to wiggle. A few seconds later... SPOINKERS WAS OFF THE GROUND!

Santa called to his reindeer, "Comet, come help out our newest flyer."

Comet and the other reindeer came quickly. To their amazement, Spoinkers was hovering about the pen. They always told him, "Pigs don't fly." Only today, THAT PIG WAS OFF THE GROUND!

Comet flew over and began giving Spoinkers some tips to help him stay right side up. Soon he was getting the hang of it, but he wasn't flying yet.

Santa said, "Spoinkers, push off with your feet and think of Christmas and your favorite memory."

Spoinkers had wonderful memories being with his pig friends on Christmas Eve. He thought of Santa flying the sleigh and before he knew it, HE WAS FLYING!

Spoinkers could hardly believe he was flying. Comet zoomed alongside him as they soared over the village to a surprised audience of pigs and reindeer.

Comet was paying so much attention to teaching that he didn't realize there was a branch in his flight path.

Comet's back hoof hit the branch. He tumbled out of control and crashed next to the barn. Spoinkers flew down and rushed to Comet's side.

Comet said he was fine but tried walking and could not. Santa hurried to Comet and said, "That doesn't look good. Let's get the doctor."

Comet was worried. He knew if he couldn't walk, then he couldn't fly, and Santa was counting on him.

Spoinkers felt confused. He was happy to have flown but sad for Comet. He felt a little responsible.

He went back to his pen, but didn't get much rest.

The next day, Santa and Comet came to see Spoinkers, who felt sadness when he saw Comet's leg in a cast.

Santa and Comet could see the worry on Spoinkers' face. They told him it wasn't his fault, and his flying was spectacular. Santa said, "Comet won't be able to pull the sleigh and since you did so well, Comet would like to train you to take his place."

Spoinkers wasn't sure he heard it right, "You want ME to pull the sleigh?"

Santa and Comet both said, "Yes, we do!" Spoinkers' dream was to pull the sleigh, although now he was getting nervous.

Comet assured Spoinkers that with his training and help from the reindeer, Spoinkers would do great.

Spoinkers couldn't say no to Santa.

So he said, "It's a beautiful day today. Not a cloud in the sky and a perfect day for a pig to learn how to fly."

Look for more stories about me.
Merry Christmas from Spoinkers and everyone at
the North Pole!

56606282R00020

Made in the USA
San Bernardino, CA
12 November 2017